The Tip of The Tale

Suzanne Alexander

illustrated by Ashley Teets

Headline Kids
an imprint of Headline Books, Inc.
Terra Alta, WV

The Tip of The Tale

by Suzanne Alexander

illustrated by Ashley Teets

copyright ©2021 Suzanne Alexander

To order additional copies of this book, or for book publishing information, or to contact the author:

Headline Kids
P. O. Box 52
Terra Alta, WV 26764

Email: mybook@headlinebooks.com
www.headlinebooks.com

Lucas Kelly—*Design/Layout*

Published by Headline Books
Headline Kids is an imprint of Headline Books

ISBN-13: 9781951556396

Library of Congress Control Number: 2020944375

PRINTED IN THE UNITED STATES OF AMERICA

This book is dedicated to my late mother, Vivian Ackerson, whose adage "reach for a star and fall short, you're still higher than if you never reached at all" has guided my life.

As the sun set below the tall trees, a red fox opened one eye and then the other.

Grumble Rumble

As he opened his mouth in a huge yawn, Fox heard
the familiar sound of "Grumble! Rumble!" coming from his
stomach. *I'm hungry!* thought Fox, *but what shall I eat?*

Ahh, a plump, juicy chicken dinner is just what I need.
Fox trotted through the forest where he saw a
barn's shiny silo in the moonlight. A *farm*, thought Fox.
There must be chickens there.

Hmm...no chickens...just a cat...
"What do you want?" growled the cat.
"Chickens!" said Fox, "Got any?"
"No chickens here!" the cat answered. "Just pigs.
Lots of pigs! And corn. Lots of corn! Try the farm
down the road."

Fox scampered as fast as he could.

"Still no chickens... but another cat?"

"What do you want!?" asked the cat.

"Chickens!" said Fox, "Got any?"

"No chickens here!" said the black cat, snarling. "Just sheep. Lots of sheep! And wool. Lots of wool! Try the farm down the road."

Fox made a quick turn.
There **must** be chickens there...

Yikes! Cats?!!
"What do you want??"
"Chickens!" said Fox, "Got any?"
"No chickens here!" yowled both cats at
once. "Just horses. Lots of horses! And hay.
Lots of hay! Try the farm down the road."
Fox gave a long sigh.

STILL NO CHICKENS!
JUST ANOTHER CAT!
"Do-you-have-any-chickens?"
asked Fox, out of breath.
"No chickens here," hissed the
cat who didn't like her washing to be
disturbed. "Just cows. Lots of cows!
And milk. Lots of milk!"

18

Milk? The milk will just have to do for now,
thought Fox. But as he lunged for the cat's bowl...

Fox ran out of the barn...

...and through the fields
of hay, grass, and corn—
back into the woods.

Shhh...

As fox began to clean himself off,
he thought, *Not a plump, juicy chicken
dinner, but not bad tasting.*

Fox licked the milk off
his paws and his shoulders,
but he couldn't reach the
milk under his chin.

And he completely forgot to lick the milk that landed on the tip of his tail.

So, if you look carefully at a red fox, you will still see the milk beneath his chin and on the very tip of his tail.

Red Fox Facts

- Red foxes are found throughout the world. They live in grasslands, forests, mountains, deserts, and even suburbs and cities.

- Usually weighing less than 15 pounds (6.8 kilograms), red foxes have long fur, bushy tails, and pointed ears and noses.

- At birth, red foxes are grey or brown. Their red coat grows in when they are about one month old. However, there are some red foxes that have golden, reddish brown, silver, or black fur. Most have the white tip at the end of their tail and white fur on their chin and chest.

- All foxes have excellent hearing, smell, and eyesight. They are nocturnal which means they are mostly active at night, especially at dawn and dusk.

- Foxes are omnivores, meaning they eat both meat and plants. Like the red fox in our story, they prefer birds and small mammals. They like to hunt alone.

- Using whines, growls, yips, and barks, foxes "talk" to each other.

- A fox is a canine, related to the dog family. Male foxes actually are called dogs; females are called vixens; and their babies are called kits or sometimes cubs or pups.

- The vixen produces a litter of 1 to 12 kits each year. Kits leave their families to go out on their own at about 7 months old. In the wild, foxes only live from 2 to 4 years.

Find More Facts About Red Foxes

- Gentle, Victor and Perry, Janet. Red Foxes. Milwaukee, WI: Gareth Stevens, Inc., 2002.

- Pringle, Laurence. The Secret Life of the Red Fox. Honesdale, PA: Boyds Mills Press, 2017.

- Red Fox. National Geographic. https//www.nationalgeographic.com/animals/mammals/r/red-fox/ January 1, 2018.

The Tip of the Tale is a beautifully illustrated story of a fox hunting for a chicken dinner at the local farms. Rebuffed by barn cats at every stop, the wily fox decides to share the cat's bowl of milk and gets a surprise from the quick-footed cat!

This wonderful tale is an excellent early reader with the added surprise of hidden chickens at every farm and includes fox facts. *The Tip of the Tale* won first place in the Children's Book Category of the West Virginia Writers' Contest as an unpublished manuscript.

"Clever chickens manage to outsmart a hungry fox in this creative and colorfully told tale by Suzanne Alexander, and she even solves the mystery of how the fox got his white-tipped tail!"

— **Laura Treacy Bentley**, author of *Sir Grace and the Big Blizzard*

Suzanne Alexander has been a docent for the Huntington Museum of Art for over twelve years as well as an outreach teacher for their Museum Making Connections program. Throughout her career as an elementary school librarian, language arts teacher, children's librarian in a public library, and book columnist, Suzanne has shared her love of reading and art. She currently writes stories and articles for children and young adults and is a member of the West Virginia Writers, Inc. and the Society of Children's Book Writers and Illustrators. Her first book, *Through Children's Eyes: Exploring the Huntington Museum of Art*, is a Gold Mom's Choice Award Winner and was selected for Creative Child Magazine's Book of the Year Award. In her free time, Suzanne enjoys traveling which often creates inspiration for her writing.

Award-winning author and illustrator, **Ashley Teets**, is a summa cum laude graduate of Alderson Broaddus College with a B.F.A. in visual art with a minor in creative writing. After two semesters of graduate work at West Virginia University, she continued her graduate study through the Simmons College satellite graduate program at the Eric Carle Museum of Picture Book Art in Amherst, Massachusetts. She holds a Masters in Arts Administration through the University of Kentucky and is a graduate of Don Bluth University. Ashley is also a portrait artist, muralist and art instructor.

Headline Kids

www.headlinebooks.com
2018 Independent Publisher of the Year

ISBN 13: 9781951556396